THE Bunny

Bill Richardson

Band

PICTURES BY

Roxanna Bikadoroff

GROUNDWOOD BOOKS
HOUSE OF ANANSI PRESS
TORONTO   BERKELEY

Groundwood Books / House of Anansi Press
groundwoodbooks.com

We acknowledge for their financial support of our publishing program the
Canada Council for the Arts, the Ontario Arts Council and the Government of Canada.

Canada Council   Conseil des Arts
for the Arts   du Canada

ONTARIO ARTS COUNCIL
CONSEIL DES ARTS DE L'ONTARIO
an Ontario government agency
un organisme du gouvernement de l'Ontario

With the participation of the Government of Canada   Canadä
Avec la participation du gouvernement du Canada

Library and Archives Canada Cataloguing in Publication
Richardson, Bill, author
The bunny band / Bill Richardson ; illustrated by Roxanna Bikadoroff.
Issued in print and electronic formats.
ISBN 978-1-77306-093-4 (hardcover).—ISBN 978-1-77306-094-1 (PDF)
I. Bikadoroff, Roxanna, illustrator II. Title.
PS8585.I186B86 2018   jC813'.54   C2017-907470-9
C2017-907471-7

The illustrations were done in ink, watercolor and colored pencil on Stonehenge paper.
Design by Michael Solomon
Printed and bound in Malaysia

MIX
Paper from
responsible sources
FSC® C012700
FSC
www.fsc.org

To Eric Friesen, bringer of music
and jollity, in abundant
and equal measure.
BR

To Sheila.
RB

Lavinia loved all vegetables.
She bought some seeds to sow.
She planted them. She watered them.
Lavinia watched them grow.
Some cabbages, some lettuces,
some radishes, some kale,
tomatoes, red as red can be,
and cauliflowers, pale.

Nice Cabbage!

But someone else loved veggies, too.
When each new morning dawned,
Lavinia, dismayed, would find
her spuds or beans were gone.

Some people!

"Who dares to come and nibble here?
Who gnaws each tender leaf?"

Lavinia, angry, set a snare
to catch the veggie thief.

At midnight, when the moon was full,
she heard a chilling shriek.
"At last!" she cried. "I've nabbed the knave
who eats my peas and leeks."
The moon shone on her garden.
She went. She looked. She saw
a white and frightened bunny
with her rope wrapped round his paw.

"Ho ho, you rogue," Lavinia said.
"Your pirate days are through.
You've stolen all my veggies,
now I'll turn you into stew."

To her surprise, the bunny spoke.
He said, "Oh, no! Oh, no!
Don't hurt me. I'll reward you,
if you'll only let me go."

"I'm not your basic bunny.
I've got magic up my sleeve.
And I will help your garden grow,
if you'll just let me leave."
"You promise?" said Lavinia.
Said the bunny, "Cross my heart."
She cut the rope. He vanished.
He was swallowed by the dark.

waste not
want not ...

Lavinia did not go to bed.
She clambered up a tree.
She waited in the moonlight,
watched to see what she might see.

There came a gentle rustling,
and Lavinia was amazed,
for all around her garden
where the veggie thief had grazed ...

there were bunnies, bunnies, bunnies,
by the dozen, by the score —
cream and tan and black and brown,
and more and more and more.

And all the bunnies gathered there
were clutching in their hands
not vegetables but instruments.
Gadzooks! A bunny band.

Lavinia watched, astonished,
as the silent, silvery moon
shone its light on mandolins,
on banjos and bassoons,

on harps and ukuleles —
it was bright, as bright as day —
trumpets, bagpipes, fifes and drums,
the band began to play.

Their music was enchanting,
not a clamor, not a din.
The robber bunny led the band
and bowed his violin.
They plucked and blew the whole night through.
When dusk gave way to dawn,
Lavinia yawned. She blinked.
She gasped. The bunny band was gone.

At dusk, the band returned again.
They played the whole night through.
That bunny kept his promises —
her garden grew and grew.
Their serenade, enchanted, made
her onions huge, like moose.
Zucchinis, far from weeny,
were the size of a caboose.

Holy moly!

Her neighbors, friends and relatives
all marveled at her luck.
Her beets and sprouts beyond all doubt
were big as two-ton trucks.

Autumn Harvest Fair

That's just nuts!

Her veggies won the ribbons
at the autumn harvest fair.
The days grew short. Lavinia thought,
"The time has come to share."

HOME
SWEET
CAVE

The bunnies turned up one last time,
and when their songs were played,
Lavinia brought them all inside.
They found her table laid

with vats of varied vegetables,
enough to feed a horse.
She sent them home with what remained,
in bunny bags, of course.

She thanked each bunny, one by one.
They hopped off down the lane.
Their chief, the thief, said, "In the spring
we'll come to play again."

So, all that winter, by her fire,
Lavinia dozed and dreamed
of veggies grand and bunny bands
and gardens, green on green.